MW01075715

# WHAT THE GUTTER TOOK FROM US

Eccentric Angel

Copyright © 2012 bunch India

All rights reserved.

ISBN: 0615706517
ISBN: 978-0615706511

# DEDICATION

This book is dedicated to the following: To my Gram'ma Josephine who was the true definition of a phenomenal woman. This dedication is for sharing your wisdom and patience, which prepared me for some of life's most difficult challenges. To my brother Curtis a.k.a "Tiger" may he R.I.P for teaching me what it meant to be a natural born leader and never a follower. To my brother Anthony a.k.a "Red Bone" may he R.I.P for giving me a sense of security as a little girl in addition to giving that moral support that was much needed as a young adult. This book is also dedicated to all the young fallen angels who lost their lives in a senseless manner. To those that suffered abuse or neglect on any level. Last but not least, to the young adults that were never given a fair chance in life to begin with.

# CONTENTS

Acknowledgments     I

1    The beginning of our world     1

2    The many faces on my block     Pg # 4

3    Something's we never get back     Pg # 7

4    See what happens when     Pg # 17

5    You better watch yo mouth     Pg # 21

6    Where thinking you cute getcha     Pg # 22

7    See what you get for snooping     Pg # 26

8    How fast life changes     Pg # 30

9    Can't turn back the hands of time     Pg # 33

10    Hear me oh lord     Pg # 35

11    From 10 to the new me     Pg# 39

# ACKNOWLEDGMENTS

First and foremost, I would like to thank God for giving me the power to believe in my passion and pursue my dreams. Before writing this book, I realized I was blessed with the gift of writing to make others aware and encourage if nothing else. This book would not have been possible without the understanding and encouragement of my Children; Tyra, Tyjon and Tyaun. To my husband for loving me enough to understand and embrace the changes in our lives which was support beyond measure. A special thanks to my mother Flora and father Curtis for having the excitement of 100 men in reference to anticipation shown during the books completion. Words cannot express my gratitude to my Aunt Charlene, Aunt Mary and cousin William for their professional advice and assistance in polishing this manuscript. I needed to also express my appreciation to Shoney K for never hesitating to share her knowledge and experiences about the publishing process which helped my process flow with ease. Giving a special thanks to my Fristers (Friend/Sister) Dionna and Sonora as well as my God-Daughter Tashayana (Tay Tay), and Son Tyjon for giving their unfiltered feedback and suggestions ensuring my vision of helping others through words was carried out. Lastly, I want take this opportunity to thank my Friend/Tattoo-Artist Jimmy for the role played in illustrating the book cover which visually expressed the sadness in what this world as we know it has come to. I thank you all and those not mentioned for believing in me and seeing the vision,even when others didn't.

# 1. THE BEGINNING OF OUR WORLD

Yep! Everybody knows me and I know everybody *and* their business too! My name is Kanata and I'm 10 years old. So let me first start off by saying; my momma has five kids that she is *NOT* raising. Just so you know; only two of us know for sure who our daddy's are, but that don't make a bit of difference because they don't come around *anyway!* My brother Jarvis is something like the daddy of the house, because he is the one who makes sure all five of us eat and keep a roof over our head. It's crazy because I be asking my big brother why momma was always crying; If you really wanna know, I was thinking Jarvis is the one who should be crying since he gotta to do everything for us. When I would ask my brother Jermaine why is momma always crying? He would always say, "Don't worry about it, momma will be fine-it's complicated grown folk stuff you wouldn't understand even if I told you".

Now with a response like that Booooiiiii YOU ALREADY KNOW, I was on a chase for answers. See, everybody who knew me called me "Nosella", because I wouldn't rest until I found *ALL* the answers, even if it wasn't my business *ummph*! If you wanted info, I was the one to come to. So I figured, what did Jermaine know, and he wondered why we like Jarvis more. He didn't know what I knew, –how could he tell me what I wouldn't understand? Plus he was never home either, so he don't know me like that. He be trippin me out always calling me lil girl. I bet he don't be calling me lil girl once my birthday come, it's in seven months and I can't wait.

Speaking of my brothers, so I won't forget to tell you; I got a total of three brothers and a sister. My sister Katurah is13, my brother Jamal is 19, Jarvis is 20 and Jermaine is 22. Even though I'm only 10, I could tell you now; there is some serious under estimating going on. I can't believe he talking bout I wouldn't understand. Now trust me I don't understand everything, but I understand Jermaine *suuuuucks! hmmmmph.* They ain't gotta tell me nothing though, cause imma find out, you betta believe that! Ya see imma find out any way because I be seeing my momma all the time when I'm outside. momma be looking sick. Her face sunk in and she all skinny and stuff. When I ask her what's wrong, and why she be having on the same clothes? she say" *ain't nothing wrong.* I know she using them drugs though cause why she don't *never* have no money; always begging my brothers. I heard her tell my brother she needed some money cause she was dope sick;

so *BOOM* to them for thinking I don't be knowing stuff. *And I know* what dope sick mean, cause yep I sholl do be listening to the boys that be shooting dice when I go to the store. All the boys talk about is selling drugs, and girls. It's this boy name Mario he *too* cute! I heard him say he just got outside and he *know* he was about to get paid cause all the cluckers dope sick about that time. Even though my momma don't live with us I be seeing her on the block sometimes. My momma never take me places; but when I see her she always give me something. I don't even be mad that she probably found or stole the stuff, because some kids momma's don't even think about them. When she about to go, she always say "remember these two things, I love you and I'm not too far away." When I was little I use to cry for her when she would leave me, but I guess I'm use to it now....

## 2. THE MANY FACES ON MY BLOCK

We stay on the Westside of Chicago right off the Ave in a three-bedroom apartment over the store, I'm glad we moved, because where we use to stay was *really* bad. Every night it was all kind *of* shooting. Girls was always fighting over boys that didn't care about neither one of them. You always saw the same girls walking up and down the street with their hair not combed, and too little clothes on thinking they are *so* cute. Now that was on a *good* day, because most of the time they would have on pajamas outside like nothing was even wrong with that. If I saw one more girl that was like 13 or 14 with tracks hanging, and  glue in all the wrong places I was just  gone die. Ooooweee! and if I saw one more girl with all kind of dumb colors in her head and a baby on their hip, I was gonna call the ghetto patrol myself! The colorful hairstyles wouldn't have looked so bad if it was done right at least.  What made it so bad was you could tell somebody that didn't know what they was doing did it for them *AND*...with the wrong kind of hair, looking like a long fat fluffy wig. I got too tired of seeing dirty old men watching lil girl's booties then have the nerve to say lil dirty old man stuff like "uhm uhm uhm." On our old block you would always see wanna-be-thugs with yellow tank tops on that *use* to be white. Standing in the same place all day and night calling they self selling drugs, but they never got nothing to show for it and you never saw them clean. Ooh I take that back, the only one you use to see clean was Maaaario -Boom! But the other ones, I bet they just use to wake up in the morning and go! now imagine how that smelled. One day one of the boys named Skully tried to talk to this girl that was going in the store, cause I told you they always in front of the same ole store; anyway He gone say "Hey lil Momma, let me get a number outcha." She turned around and said "For the last three days I've walked past the store, you had those same clothes on." Then she said "Now why would I want to give you my number?" Guess what he said; he gone say" lil momma I'm grinding, these just my hustling clothes." I was thinking eeeewwwww, for three days though -Really! I gotta look up what grind mean for real because grind gotta mean same dirty and nasty clothes on for three days. I can't even repeat what he called her when she made it in the store. You know how I heard all of that? Because, I was sitting on the porch next door to the store. I was even listening to these girls argue. They had the same baby daddy, and to tell you the truth; I don't think neither one of the babies was his. Where we stay now, is just how it was where we use to stay; errrrbody know me. People on the block be wanting me to sit on their porch and tell them all the juicy news. I gotta real good view, because we stay like four houses from the corner and my room is right in the front. Now you see why I'm so glad we moved, and we moved right in time for my birthday. Jamal said he's gonna throw me a big party. Momma said she would, but I'm still waiting on the other nine parties she promised me... HA! I bet I won't be holding my breath waiting on it, or I'll pass out for sure. Momma never do stuff like that, Jamal always gotta do it.

# 3 SOMETHINGS WE NEVER GET BACK

Even Jarvis said momma still going through some stuff, That's why she don't do as much as she should for us. My momma had a rough life, but I never knew just how rough until now. See I found out why it was so rough, and why she was always crying. My Gram'ma had nine kids, five boys and four girls. My momma was the middle child. She always felt like she was alone and had to fight for attention. She said when she was my age she dreamed of getting married and having two kids; *nuh uh*, we see that married part didn't happen *and* momma's math was off about the two kids part too. She said she wanted to be a Pediatrician. She always wanted to help people who couldn't help themselves, and the ones that probably wasn't being treated right by others. Who knew she was talking about herself.

From what I heard, my Momma was always forgotten about

since she was the middle child. I know that had to suck, and since nobody really was there to watch out for momma; something happened to her that changed her life forever.

Since Jarvis or Jermaine wouldn't tell me why momma was always crying I told you I was gone find out *AND I DID...HELLO!* I was over my friend CeCe house, she stay down the street from my Gram'ma. Right next to CeCe house is an abandoned building; my momma and her friend be sitting over there all the time. One day they was laughing about stuff that use to happen in the old days, but it didn't last long cause momma said she could only remember a few good things that happened to her, but I bet she could remember all of the bad stuff. That was my cue, so you know I was right in that window *LISTENING*. Momma was telling her friend when she was little, a friend of Gram'mas named Uncle Hank use to come over to their house, and every time he came over there he would always say "Look at my lil pretty niece, Kerri." He would always tell her "You're gonna be a heartbreaker." Since nobody really never paid her no attention she said she use to like when he came over. Momma said one time he came to their house looking for my Gram'ma, but she wasn't at home. He asked momma where everybody was; She told him Gram'ma was at work like she always was, and everybody else was outside. He said he was about to go and asked if he could get a hug, but he took more than that. momma said she was messed up every since; oh I forgot to tell you she was only 12 at the time. When momma got to talking about that part she started crying and I was like Johnny on the spot! I ran down the stairs; skipping stairs and all to hear momma's story, and to get the info I always knew I was gonna find out BOOM!. When momma was telling the story, she started to cry even harder. She asked how I knew she was down there. I told her I was in the window the whole time. She said, "You wasn't suppose to know any of that" and I replied," momma how do you expect me to know how to stop stuff like this from happening to me if my own momma not teaching me nothing?" Momma's tears fell even more; she stopped to catch her breath then momma said, what happened to her was one of the main reasons why she didn't trust many people. I was thinking in my head, momma if you *reeeeeally* didn't trust people why we all got different daddies. Then I laughed under my breath; by that time momma's friend snuck off the porch. I'm thinking "TOO Petty" cause she didn't wanna hear momma's sad story she just eased off the porch, it was kinda funny how she did it though. Momma just kept on talking and I loved every minute of it!

Listening to momma tell her story, had me in a daze. It was like I was there. She said when she was growing up, she wasn't fast or nothing because of what happened to her when she was 12. She was just turning 16 when she got her first boyfriend. Momma said he was really sweet, but talked real slick. She told me when I grow up I gotta be really careful cause boys that talk real slick could talk you right out of, or right into *almost* anything. I understand now why she tried to warn me. Since Momma was alone all the time as a kid, all she really did was read book after book. She said she used to read nothing but fairytales because in fairytales there was always a happy ending. One day she said she was walking down the street to the library like she always did, but this time was different. She had her head down, because she was just about finished reading her book; when a tall brown-skinned man bumped right into her. Not knowing what to do, she apologized falling forward right into his arms. The feeling that came over her was nothing like she had ever felt before. As crazy as it sounds, she said she felt really safe in his arms; reminding her of something she had read before. He asked Momma her name and she said it flew right out of her mouth. Seems like momma didn't only like reading, turns out she was liking on a dude name Rio. From the time Momma bumped into Rio, she was hoping that he would be by the library every time she went to return a book. Momma said when she saw him her eyes lit up, and it felt like butterflies was in her stomach. She said even though she was nervous then, after seeing him in the neighborhood so much; she felt like she knew him for a long time. Momma said after a short time passed, whenever she saw him it was a rush that she loved. At first when he would say stuff to her, she would be so scared. She said she would just smile and get stuck, but as time passed she was able to answer him without being nervous. She said he brought her right out of her shell, whatever that means—anyway; they started seeing each other every day. They talked about almost everything, but she felt like it was something he wasn't telling her. The more they were around each other, the more it seemed like it was something about him that wasn't right. They would go out sometimes and because Momma had never been anywhere but in her neighborhood, nobody really knew her outside the neighborhood. Now the funny thing was, everywhere they went *everybody* knew Rio and he knew everybody. Momma said even though she had a feeling that something wasn't right about him; it still was something about him that made her feel so safe and loved.

Momma said she never asked where he worked or nothing since they were the same age, plus he was always hanging around her the neighborhood so she thought he didn't have a job. He said he had family who stayed a couple of blocks away from Gram'ma; so to momma that explained why he was always in the neighborhood.

Now since momma didn't really go outside or have many friends, Rio really could have just told momma anything. She said she remembered everything like it was yesterday, and that's why she cried so much now. Momma said the pain is still there. They had been going together for three months and you can say he was her first because what her so-called uncle did to her didn't count. She said Rio use to wait on her to come outside everyday; they even read some of the same books, talking about them for hours. Momma never heard anything bad about him and Rio always made her feel like she was the only girl in his life, or at least that's what she thought. Momma said every day she started noticing the same girl come around at the same time. He told momma that girl was his cousin who had to live with them because her mother died when she was little. Rio told her she had to bring him his key every day before their Gram'ma left for work so they wouldn't be locked out. Momma said his cousin was always looking sad when she came around, but she never said too much or never really even looked at momma. Momma said it really didn't seem odd since all her brothers and sisters didn't have their own keys to the house either. Anyway momma said he really was like her prince charming in the beginning, but then she said after a while the sweet things he use to tell her wasn't happening that much anymore. Then he just stopped coming around all together. What momma didn't know is that, that was all part of the game he would play to get girls to do just what he wanted. Momma said when she called him, his girl cousin would always say he wasn't around or that he would call her back. Momma said she cried every day because she didn't know what was going on. A couple of days turned into a week of not talking to Rio or seeing him. She never remembered any other time in her life feeling that alone. Nobody knew what was wrong with momma cause she wouldn't talk to nobody, she said all she did was cry. It was going into the second week of no Rio. With momma hurting so bad; the only thing that made her feel a little better was reading, and that's what she did. Momma built up enough energy to go to the library, and I don't even have to tell you who she saw walking her way. You already know, it was Rio lil dirty butt. Momma said she didn't know how to feel. She said she wanted to be mad cause he just stop coming around, but she missed him so much; she said all she could do was cry and keep walking. She tried to walk past him, but he grabbed her hand and pulled her close to hug her. She said she wanted to push him away but that lonely feeling instantly went away once she felt his hug. She said that hug warmed her soul, when she said that I was thinking *no wonder every time momma tell her story her friend take off.* Who wanna hear that over soft stuff? Momma said they walked to the park behind the library cause he said he really needed to talk to her. He said he had something really important to tell her. Once they made it to the park; they sat far behind by the trees, cause he said he didn't want nobody to see him. He told her even though he told her almost everything, one thing he didn't tell her was that he gambled a lot and owed somebody a lot of money. Rio told momma if he didn't pay back the persons money he messed up he would have to move out of town for good. Momma asked if he could get the money from his Gram'ma, and he said his Gram'ma only got her disability check that she had to pay the rent with. Rio told momma he didn't have anybody to get it from. Momma was sad cause she couldn't handle the thought of the best thing that had ever happened to her having to leave her for good. He said there was only one way to clean up the debt he owed, so momma was happy thinking she was about to hear good news. He said the person he owed said he used to see him and momma by the library and thought momma was really pretty. The man said if momma went to the drive-in with him one time Rio's debt would be considered paid. Momma didn't want to do it but couldn't imagine her life without Rio, so she said she would do it. Rio said he wouldn't be far away and as soon as the movie was over he would be right there to get Momma. After she said ok Rio said he had to get ready to go before somebody saw him. Rio told Momma he would meet her by the library the next day at 5 o'clock. So she said she went home and went to bed without telling anybody what had just happened. The next day came and just as planned, Momma said she met Rio at the library at 5 o'clock on the dot. As soon as she made it there she saw Rio pulling around the corner by the park. Momma didn't know the man would be waiting too. When momma saw them momma told me she was scared, but Rio told her don't worry cause he would be right behind them. Momma said all types of stuff was running through her mind, and all she wanted to do was get it over with. Momma said she pulled Rio to the side and told him she didn't have a good feeling about going with the man, and didn't want to do it. Rio said "I thought you loved me and didn't want me to move" Momma said she told him " I do love you and I don't want you to have to go." Rio said he knew momma was just lil nervous and he had something for her to take so she won't be so nervous, he told Momma it would be over before she knew it. She said Rio had a really small square of aluminum foil and in it was some whitish-brown powder. He told momma to close her eyes and take a deep breath. "After that, momma said she remembered blanking in and out only remembering Rio putting her in the man's car and whispering in her ear he was "right behind them." After what seemed like a long time, in her cloudy head all she could remember was the man taking off her clothes; because of what Rio gave her she was too out of it to fight him off." Momma said once she woke up she remembered screaming and crying telling Rio they didn't see no movie and all she remembered was the man taking her clothes off and forcing his self in her. She said instead of Rio making her feel safe he called her all types of names and said all she was suppose to do is go to the movies with him not have sex with him. Momma cried more screaming "he raped me!" but Rio blamed everything on her and told her "You are damaged goods." He told her the only way he would mess with her is if she paid him. Momma really didn't trust Rio or nobody else after that, because she already couldn't forget what my Gram'mas friend did to her and the one other time she trusted a man he ended up hurting her too. That was the start of momma's life on drugs and all the other stuff she do now.

My Gram'ma told me my momma was leaving with a different man every night and the result of that was all five of us. So, now you know why some of us didn't know who our daddies was. If you didn't catch that, momma was a hooker. Surprised huh? I couldn't believe it either. It turns out momma's first boyfriend was a pimp who liked to trick women and make them sale their bodies. Come to find out that girl cousin of Rio's was really another one of his hookers who he did the same thing to. That's what kind of pushed my momma over the edge. And my brother Jermaine gone say, I wouldn't understand. What's so hard to understand? momma was abused by people she trusted and turned out to be a drug addicted hooker. I get it.

## 4. SEE WHAT HAPPENS WHEN...

Speaking of Jermaine, it didn't seem like he was any better. He was in and out the house all day. He really think I don't know he sale drugs. Now don't this sound like a drug dealer. He use to dress real fly, changed cars like he changed girls and had a shoe box full of money that he thought I didn't know about. What sucked is for him to be the oldest brother; he never did anything for us either. Every time we would ask him for some money, his famous words was "ain't no money." On the other hand there was my brother Jarvis. Now he sold drugs too, but for some reason it was different. The difference between the two was my oldest brother Jermaine was all about looking out for his self and others who didn't really give a crap about him, but Jarvis was always looking out for everybody else more than he looked out for his self. Jermaine didn't really talk to us or make sure we were okay since momma was never there but Jarvis *always* did. Like I said before, he was always in and out; so it was like we really didn't know Jermaine. I know that sounds messed up, but it's the truth. That's why since it was all about him, it blew up in his face. Gram'ma says, "You gotta be careful who you turn your back on, because one day you just might end up needing them" and that's so true. It was true, because one day my brother was coming from picking up a whole lot of drugs and somebody must have told on him because he ended up in a high speed chase. While the police was chasing him, he peed on his self or at least that's what I heard.

Now he didn't care nothing about us so why should we care about him. See Jarvis is the one who got the call that Jermaine was in jail. He's been in there for two months so you know he ain't never getting out. He call like every day, sometimes I just look at the phone and let it ring. He keep calling back to back saying stuff real fast, when he know he just should be saying his name. When he do catch Jarvis at home he be asking Jarvis to send him some money. He be wanting Jarvis to give his so called lawyer  thousands of dollars, he think the lawyer can get him out of jail. He got the nerve to want us to come see him. I say, "What about all the girlfriends he had, where they at ?" because of how Jarvis is, he always make us go. He says no matter how Jermaine was to us, we family and we all we got. I guess he right. When we do go visit, we have to talk through a thick glass with little holes in it, and it always smell like breath. Jermaine be talking about what we better not be doing. Go figure, Jermaine is in jail he wants to be a big brother, but who he think gonna listen? Jarvis tell us to give him a chance. Jarvis said sometimes it takes a person to go through something to become a better person .we'll see how that goes.

## 5. YOU BETTA WATCH YO MOUTH

Even though Jarvis is only 20, he is more like the man of the house, so we listen to what he say. Not just cause we are scared of him, but cause he got a whole lot of love for us. Katurah didn't like him, but I loved him. Any time Katurah said something wrong about him, I would say, "Shut up! You lucky he look out for us." And all the time Katurah would say "I can't stand Jarvis he think he our Daddy when he a kid his self." I would say, "You should be glad since you don't even know who yo Daddy is." Thinking; hi five to myself, with a huge smile on my face. Then I would say in my head," that should teach her to be talking crazy about Jarvis".

## 6. WHERE THINKING YOU CUTE GETCHA

I told you my sister Katurah is only 13 but she be thinking she too cute. She got long black hair, and she is not shaped like a 13 year old either. She shaped more like a 20 year old. She be trying to wear makeup, and be looking like a big clown. She always sneaking out the house every chance she gets, even though she know Jarvis is gonna get her when she come home. She say his whippings don't be doing nothing, that's why she still sneak out. Jarvis be telling her" if she keep trying to be grown she gonna get herself in something she can't get out of." One time she left the house without permission, and was talking to a boy in front of the house. She was leaning in his car laughing and giggling. What she didn't know was Jarvis was standing right on the sidewalk right behind her fast butt. Her giggles stopped when that brick hit that boy's car. The boy didn't even say nothing, cause he knew if he did he was probably gonna get hurt.

Some people be acting like they too scared of Jarvis. If something ever happened to one of Jarvis' friends, he was always the first person they would call. I didn't like it much though, because I always felt like his friend was always calling him when they got into some mess; he might be the one that ends up getting hurt. Anytime something did happen, he would get on the phone, and before you knew it a million boys would be at our house. I get sad when I think about something ever happening to Jarvis, because he is the best brother in the world. When I start thinking like that I just switch up my thoughts and start thinking about how my party gonna be. I really think Jarvis in a gang though, because I already know he sell drugs and like I said, all it take is one phone call and too many cars pull up. Even though I think he in a gang, he always telling us we shouldn't be around people in gangs. He said if momma was able to buy the things he needed for school, or he knew who his father was; he would have never stopped going to school. He even told us when we get married it should be to a man who don't sell drugs or be in and out of jail. Jarvis was always nice and sweet to us. He was always trying to teach us to do the right thing, even if we didn't want to do it. He didn't even curse around us. He would say "I better not catch y'all cursing, because that's a sign of a small vocabulary. He would say, "If you can't hold a real conversation without half of the words being curse words why would somebody wanna even listen." Every time he would say that, Katurah would throw up her middle finger when his back was turned.

Katurah got a lot of nerve, acting like that. Did she forget momma or Jermaine is never at home and when they are, it's not like they do anything for us. That's the main reason Jarvis dropped out of school, because he already know how momma sent him to school. He got tired of momma trying to make him go to school in tight pants that flooded all across the land. He didn't even get to go to no high school stuff like dances or trips. So he just said forget it and stopped going to school. When Jarvis first started selling drugs he would be gone all the time, but he always made sure he checked on me, Katurah  and Jamal. It was like we really didn't have a mother. We didn't see her for days sometimes. Plus she was always high off drugs and if we had any money lying around, we could forget it. To tell you the truth; I cry a lot when she's not around, because I worried about if she's okay or not when she be in the streets. I even worry about if one day something happens to her and she never come home. Momma and Jarvis would fight sometimes, because he said momma be stealing his stuff, so he got a big lock on his door. He said I'm his little spy. He give me money to watch his room, because momma be stealing his money, Jamal and Katurah be stealing his clothes. So you know, I be getting paid. Jarvis be having too much money, and he don't mind sharing it.

# 7. SEE WHAT YOU GET FOR SNOOPING

Even though momma is never at home, and Jarvis be gone sometimes, it's not so bad since we got Jamal. My brother Jamal is kind of different from other boys. He's like a second mother to us. He cooks, cleans, and takes us shopping when Jarvis gives us money. Jamal doesn't talk a lot, but we could talk to him about *anything*. Jamal never really had a lot of friends and we never saw him with a girl. I wonder why, because I gotta give my bro his props, he was a cutie. We must've had the same daddy because you gotta know I'm a lil cutie too *HELLO*! Like I said before; my brother Jamal didn't talk a whole lot, but he wrote in this little black book all the time. He was really smart and knew a lot of big words, so some of the things he said you probably couldn't understand either. He didn't talk to many people because he said people can be cruel sometimes.

One day I peeked at what he was writing, but guess what? You already know I didn't understand not none of it. When Jamal is around us he seems so happy, but I don't think he is happy for real. You know why I say that, cause one day I was snooping around his room and found the little black book that he always use to write in. In that book you would think he was a different person. He talked about feeling out of place and not being accepted, and I was thinking to myself "What is he talking about?" He said people use to call him a queer when he would walk pass, like he couldn't hear them. That's messed up people would do that. *Now* all I had to do was figure out what a queer is. You know when I don't know something I have to find out, so I looked up queer in the dictionary. Now I told you before my brother was different from other boys but now it's confirmed. If you haven't figured it out yet, *YEP* my brother is gay.

Some people may have a problem with that, but I don't. I don't see him any different than I always did, he still takes good care of us. The only time Jamal would really talk to us was when he was combing our hair. He would always tell me to be proud of who I am and never give up on what I believe in. I remember one time when he was combing Katurah hair, he said "Katurah in your life you have to stand for something or you will fall for anything" Jamal be saying stuff sometime that go right over my head cause I don't understand what he be meaning by it. He said, "We have to stick together and stay strong, since it's so much crazy stuff in this world we have to deal with." See again I didn't know what he was talking about because, even though I don't have a momma and Daddy in the same house, I'm still happy. I'm even happier when I go over my Gram'ma's house, cause she make me oatmeal and toast with butter on each corner and one butter spot in the middle. Gram'ma tucks me in at night and lets me watch TV all night until I fall asleep. Gram'ma don't know all the stuff that goes on at home, cause Jarvis say "What goes on here stays here." He say, "Everybody shouldn't know our business" and I be smiling cause I don't tell our business but I sholl be telling everybody else's.

Today is gonna be a good day because you know what today is? You know, it's my birthday right? Oh yeah, oh yeah, I see Jamal putting up my decorations and I can't wait. Hold on one minute, you know I'm being nosey looking out my window, because I just heard too many shots down the street somewhere. Now I'm hearing too many people screaming.

# 8. HOW FAST LIFE CHANGES

I know I haven't been talking like I use to, but I know you know why. I just can't believe somebody's life could change so fast. I was waiting on what I thought would be the happiest day of my life but now I wish that day had never come. I cry every night, because of what happened. Katurah hadn't been right since. My sister thought she couldn't stand Jarvis but now she sees what he was trying to prevent from happening. She needed him more than she thought, now she wishes she could take back everything mean she ever said about him. Since we wasn't close to Jermaine it didn't bother us, but to lose Jarvis hurt so bad.

Oh I forgot to tell you what happened to my sister. She started staying out all night sometimes she was drinking liquor and trying different drugs, because she thought it would make the pain go away. But I guess it didn't, it end up bringing more pain. Katurah said one night she had been smoking weed and drinking, thinking that was somehow gonna help her stop thinking about what happened to Jarvis, because she said she felt guilty. She would always tell my Gram'ma it was all her fault. Remember when I said I heard a lot of screaming, I heard my sister's screams the loudest when it all happened. If I was Katurah, I probably would have felt like it was my fault too. Since she thought it was her fault she would always be gone. She was running from her pain and ended up running into something else. One day around 2 o'clock in the morning she was coming from the park. She didn't think nothing of it since the park was only a block away from the house. She noticed a man following her, and she said she started walking faster and so did he. Before she could run, he grabbed her and pulled her in a dark alley, then he raped her. Gram'ma be trying to take us to talk to people, but I don't wanna talk. I just want to wake up from this nightmare, or at least I wish it was just a nightmare. At first I didn't understand what Jamal meant by some of the things he use to say, but I understand now. What I mean by that is, I liked to visit Gram'ma, but I never thought we would end up having to live with her. I'm tired of crying but, I can't stop thinking about what happened. I just keep seeing it over and over when I'm in school and every single night when I try to go to sleep. I keep seeing Jarvis crawling up the stairs covered in blood. Blood was coming out of his mouth and tears was coming from his eyes. I talk to God and ask him to help me understand why he had to take my brother but I guess I am just a kid who doesn't understand complicated grown folk stuff. Remember when I said that boy Katurah was talking to, when Jarvis threw that brick; I guess he wasn't scared of my brother after all. It was a lot of crazy stuff going on, and to top it off, everybody has something they want to talk about like my jerk brother Jermaine for starters. Now we have to go see this jerk of a brother in jail so let's see just see what he has to say. He better be lucky his old girl friend still keep in touch with us because we could care less about going to see him, especially with Jarvis being gone all. Plus, Jermaine hasn't changed; It's still all about him. So I guess we'll head in this jail and see what script he has to tell...

# 9. CAN'T TURN BACK THE HANDS TIME

You just don't know how good it is to see you. I expected you not to answer my calls, but what I didn't expect was to see you here. To be honest I didn't expect anyone to show up, but I'm glad you two came. I learned early in my 10- year bit to expect the unexpected but I still didn't expect for you to come with my brother and sister. Can I ask what made you come, Considering how I treated you when we were together? Never mind why, but I wanted to thank you whatever the reason was. I never got a chance to tell you how much I appreciated the fact that you never turned your back on my brothers and sisters at a time when I should have been there for them the most. I thought I would never be able to have a peaceful night of sleep after I found out about what happened to my little brother Jarvis and sister Katurah. One thing I know is if you eventually allow your higher being in, he will help you deal with the pain, but the guilt haunts you daily. I'm just grateful I have the chance to try to make amends with you all. Some would say I can't blame myself for the tragedies that came upon our family, but when I think about how many times I brushed my sisters and brothers off, I can't help but to blame myself somewhat. I remember when Kanata was about 8; she would always try to ask me questions, to try and understand what was going on with Momma, and I always brushed her off. It was no wonder my other sister ended up in the situations she did, partly because I was never there. I hate the fact that my sister witnessed me disrespecting women, by using them one after another. I can't even begin to count how many women I hurt. As you already know I wasn't there for Jamal so I don't know if that contributed to his way of life or not. And I know you're wondering how a misdemeanor, turned into life huh? After I got out for the misdemeanor, not even a week later I got the opportunity to avenge my brother's death by making dude pay for what he did to my lil brother. Well it was actually the most guilt of all that landed me in this horrible place I now call home. When I found out about Jarvis's death, it felt like someone had snatched my heart out my chest. He shouldn't have had to raise my sisters and other brother by himself. Then to find out how it happened devastated me even more, because I should have been there to protect him. I don't even want to begin to imagine what he was thinking while he was taking his last breath. I know it was a stupid way of thinking but at the time I felt I had to make dude pay for what he did so I made sure his family felt what mine did. I now realize that retaliation was stupid and the biggest mistake I ever made. Killing shorty made things worse, because now I really can't be there for my sister and brother. Taking dudes life was stupid, because it's not like killing him would've brought Jarvis back from the dead. What's even worse is I never once thought about the pain I caused dude kids and the fact that they had nothing to do with none of this. I should've been there for my family, man if I could just turn back the hands of time. What's even crazier is I haven't even heard from Momma in too long and that's even killing me. So how is she doing anyway? ...Why are you all looking at each other like that...and why did you all get silent?

# 10. HEAR ME OH LORD

I hate that Jermaine had to find out Momma almost died of an overdose the way he did, but that's what happens when you're not around your family. On another note; I'm excited to fill you in on my life or at least the little left that my lil nosey sister Kanata didn't tell you. Well you already know the traumatic issues that added to our screwed up situation, but I had an extra situation that magnified the extent of my stress. If you hadn't put it together with everything that Kanata told you, yes I am gay and proud of it. The reason I am so proud is because I love myself. I have a lot of people who love me for me; however, there are still so many critics in this world which is sad. As you know, I didn't end up living a life that a man is expected to live; *Honey* believe me when I tell you my life was hell in itself. The worst incident that I could remember was when I was 19. I already had to deal with the death of my brother and with my little sister being raped; in addition to having to deal with the unknown since our lives drastically changed without warning. That transition was so hard for me to understand, because I didn't have the maturity at the time to understand that things happened in life that we may never understand.

One thing I found out being a homosexual male is that there were critics that felt as though I wasn't a child of God because of my lifestyle; not understanding the only true choice that I felt I had was if I should hide who I am or be proud of who I am. I on the other hand felt like if my sexuality is something that is not of God I knew that the only option was to stay in prayer and ask my God to make the changes that he saw fit in order for my step to be in His Word. A man once told me faith without work is dead, so I continued to work to help others and I continue to pray for understanding. One thing I know is although my sexuality is not pleasing according to the bible; I know that if I didn't have anyone else God still kept me. How I know this is, reflecting back on the horrific period in my life when I had trouble coping with losing my brother; I would always catch the El to a peaceful beach up North. I couldn't have imagined going from the beach watching the waves flow to the hospital bed needing assistance breathing, because of the ignorance and unwillingness of people to accept others for who they are. While leaving the El platform, I notice some guys talking extremely loud. I couldn't help but notice the guys were making some very cruel and vulgar comments, directing them towards me. I ignored them and tried to get as far away from them as I could, but the way the platform was made; my only option was going down the stairs. Once I made it downstairs; I ended up by the park surrounded by water, in a secluded area where there were hardly any other people around. I chose to walk by the park because I thought if something happened, maybe someone riding or walking pass could come to my aid. It was very unfortunate for me that I lived in such a world where some didn't value life and was pretty heartless. Unbelievably I was chased down like an animal and beat unconscious. I was left for dead. Always wondering, if the guys that committed this senseless act had developed a conscious; the reason they didn't push me in the water to finish the demonic act they had started. If the guys were caught that brutally me; they would have been charged with a hate crime, and if they pushed me in the water and I survived it would've then been attempted murder. All I could think while this was happening to me; is how is it any human could just stand by and watch another person get beat and leave them for dead, as though they're not someone's possible son or brother. When I recovered from what could have been the end of my life I realized it was only the beginning .That incident started me on my crusade to create a safe haven for teens that are struggling with their sexuality. I wanted to create an environment that allows the attendees to feel safe while dealing with some of the many issues they may face as a result of living in this cruel and judgmental world. So that's what's been happening since the last time we spoke. Hey could you hold on for a moment? --Thanks for holding. I was just about to catch you up on what's been happening with Jermaine, and lo and behold that was him on the line. He was checking to see if we were still taking that drive to see him. Girl, thirsty is not the word for how he is when it comes to somebody, anybody visiting him. I told him I was on the line with you, and considering you've had the same number all these years --okay I just heard a pause is that your line beeping now? If so I may not have spoken soon enough. Now you see what I mean about the thirsty thing, if I just told you I was on the other line with someone, would you call them within a second of me telling you that? Ms. Lady I wouldn't answer if I were you. You may as well take that ride with us, because if he's calling your line, you may have to get that good number changed. Don't get me wrong, Jermaine has come a long way but trust me, he still has some ways to go. Honey if you answer his call one time that is all she wrote. Jermaine will call you multiple times in the same day and will have the nerve to ask you to click over and call someone else on three-way as if he has a platinum card linked to your phone line. And I bet since you didn't answer the first time, I can guarantee that's him beeping in again. So are you coming or not?

## 11. FROM 10 TO THE NEW ME

Since my little sister was so nosey and she was use to telling everybody business, I just thought this was the perfect time to share my own story since she's occupied at the moment. I'm sure you know by now my name is Katurah since my little sister told you everything else about us I'm sure. I just wanted to say how much I appreciated you lending an ear to my sister when she needed it the most. See I was never what a big sister should've been, and it was impossible to set an example for my lil sister Kanata, because I didn't know any better myself. Even though my brother tried to protect us; sometimes we think we know everything already, and end up facing some of the things I had to. I already know it's so many others besides me that thought certain things can't happen to them but, they're so wrong.

Imagine if you had to walk in my shoes, it was rough because I was a lost child that didn't have a clue, but I thought I knew everything. How do you think you would feel being raped which is a violation in itself, only to find out that you have something you can't give back. Because I thought the ultimate outcome of me being raped was so unfair, I chose to keep silent and not take advantage of the counseling that was offered to help me deal with everything that happened to me. I didn't even take into consideration how many others I may have been able to help. At one point in my life I just wanted to forget about the part I played in preventing others from living what some would consider a normal life. I thought I could really keep my secret from the rest of the world, or at least that's what I was foolish enough to have thought. I thought I was still running from my pain not realizing how deep my pain ran through me. No matter how I thought I was getting away with some of the things I should have been honest with others about, I realized your past will hunt you down for real. My secret followed me in the worst way.

I always looked older than I truly was, and guys use to say things like "Man she thicker than a snicker" every time I walked pass. I made sure my pants hugged every curve I had because I loved any attention I got. Thinking back on my life there was a period when I was having sex with 3 different guys. I felt like, because my life was a whirl wind that kept throwing me one blow after another, I had the right to live how I wanted to. I figured my mother was never a mother. I didn't know who my father was. The only man that tried to protect me, I disrespected and took him for granted not realizing until it was too late. So it seemed like I had nothing to lose. I figured; who I was hurting, it's sad it took what it did for me to realize just who I was truly hurting.

Well needless to say I ended up getting pregnant and didn't know who my baby's father was. How is that for history repeating itself? It could have been the first, second, or third guy's baby. I have to say that one of the guys always insisted on using a condom, but it still could've been his because there was one time the condom broke. If you think that was wild, it gets worse. I was on a-self-destructive war path with myself. I was now, what I heard others talking about- a baby having a baby. I didn't even have sense enough to go to the doctor even though my granny tried so hard to be there for me, and teach me the right way to go. I had it all figured out. I was going to let all three of men I was sleeping with think they were the father. I figured at least one of them was eventually going to stop messing with me anyway when I broke the news I was pregnant. I said I was just going to keep my fingers crossed and hope the one that decided to leave wasn't my baby's real father. Whichever two stuck around would be led to believe they were both the father. I just knew it would be easier to play it that way, even though I was playing Russian Roulette with all our lives. How I saw it, I needed help with my baby; so that was my only option. My attitude was, it was too late to beat myself up about not using protection at that point. All throughout my pregnancy I lied and told the guys I was going to prenatal appointments and routine doctor visits. I ended up living with one of the guys, and told the others they couldn't come over my house because my grandmother was mean and wouldn't let me have company. In the mean time I was still sleeping with all three guys. It's amazing how we sometimes make decisions before thoroughly thinking it through. I made the decision to lead all three of these guys on without even thinking for a second what may have happened if one of them found out the cruel game I played with their lives; all because I was too selfish to take their feelings into consideration. Even though I was young and naïve, I still was taught right from wrong. In some cases we should just know better than to do certain things. I should have had sense enough to know that one day my secret would eventually be revealed. As you can see from how my little sister was, there was no such thing as your business staying your business. So, I guess you're wondering how my secret hit the fan huh. Well, when I was in labor word traveled fast and because of that, all three guys showed up at the hospital. Even though two of them were able to be ruled out as being my baby's father, it still wasn't a victory to be celebrated. I gave birth to a beautiful baby girl. She was my angel, but the sad part is, she was not 100 percent healthy. I found out in the hospital that I was HIV positive because I wasn't going to prenatal appointments, nor did I get tested. Had I been more responsible, I would've known there were preventive measure I could've done once I found out I was HIV positive to decrease the chances of my little girl contracting the disease. I found out not only was my baby girl positive; so was the two guys that didn't press the issue about using protection, how disturbing is that? How many times have you heard, I *wish I would have known then what I know now?* If I had known then what I know now, I'm sure I wouldn't have ruined other lives like I did. Even though I had been raped and lost my brother, I didn't realize I still had a chance to live a productive life. I finally understood, I can't erase the past. I then realized it's not about what I can't do being HIV positive, it's more about what I can do to help others not to have to go through what I went through . My goal is to keep the channel open for our youth, letting our children of the future know that no matter what you may be going through, there's hope. I'm just trying to give them something I didn't take advantage of in hopes of stopping this vicious cycle. I am now working at my sister's non -profit-organization raising awareness. In hopes of preventing some of the things I experienced, that contributed to me making all the wrong choices. Speaking of making the wrong choices, Kanata did tell you how she ended up with the organization right? If not I can tell you. From what I understand; she ended up bumping into somebody from our old neighborhood at a stop the violence event. She said when she saw him she instantly knew who it was, and it was love at first sight. He told her he was in and out of jail for selling drugs as a little boy; until someone gave him a second chance. By him having a second chance that prompted him to want to give back to the community, to give some other lost child the same second chance he was given. They met that day eventually getting married and starting Restoration Location nonprofit organization. I didn't even tell you who the guy was; maybe you know him because she still says his name like she did back then, his name is Maaaario.

# THOUGHTS FROM THE AUTHOR

*{Getting our mind in the GUTTER to truly get out the GUTTER}*

Now my interpretation of the word "gutter" may be different on so many levels in comparison to how others may interpret it. I feel it's not just the term alone that makes the term gutter so profound; it is how the term gutter relates to you on an individual level. According to the American Heritage Dictionary of Idioms the term Gutter is defined as: "to or from squalid, degraded condition and or filthy waste. An antonym for the phrase (out of the gutter) was defined as "away from vulgarity. According the Collins English dictionary and collected by the free online dictionary defines the term gutter as a misfortune resulting in the loss of effort or money."

I personally can see the gutter as being a way of thinking that results to an action that causes pain. When it's all said and done, we will all be able to be in agreement with one another; no matter what our social class may be. We all have a gutter of our own in some way. There are things that bind us together although there is no apparent relation. When we lose someone in a violent and/or senseless way, we hurt. When we sacrifice and it seems like the light at the end of the tunnel is never coming, we hurt. When we are accustomed to a certain way of life and have to drastically adapt to something totally different without warning or preparation, we hurt. When we can't provide for ourselves or our children, we hurt.

Our society as we know it has been given an artificial illusion of power over so many of our households. That illusion of power leads to our youth's innocence being snatched away as if they never had a childhood. Because parenting didn't come with a manual, it makes us susceptible to certain situations that may put our pride, dignity, security and safety at risk.

To truly understand the complexities of this give or take relationship in reference to our vicious cycle. You must first understand the true value of what is realistically being given or taken, by what some of us may know as the gutter. Keep in mind, I'm opening this window for you to see what really happens in our society holistically ; to break this vicious cycle. In these heart breaking events; there may have been different key players involved, but the fact still remains there were heavy prices to pay. One thing's for certain, when the gutter is ready to collect; there is always something precious that is taken away from us that we just-can't-get-back...

# Message to my people

In so many cases senseless acts has contributed to our children being motherless or fatherless. Let's not forget the actions that sadly but often contributes to our parents without their children. We must not downplay how our siblings may feel when they have to take a loss. A loss is a loss whether it's drugs, death or jail that caused the break-up of our homes, the fact remains it still hurts.

Although the story you read is fiction, you must understand in so many of our homes this is reality. Don't get it twisted, I'm not insinuating the street is the cause of our screwed up situations but is a major contribution to our troubles. If we don't wake up and educate ourselves on how to talk to our children, giving them the quality time they need, there will be more and more stories just like the one you just read only they will be real. The only difference between this book and the other books to come is, the stories just may be an eye opener to some things going on in either your life or someone you know. Let's make a breakthrough restoring what was once taken from us. I've given you illustrations of the problems, the reason for the problems, and the solution. Now what are you going to do to restore what the gutter once took from us.

# _Did you know?_

❖ Children who have been victims of sexual abuse exhibit long-term and more frequent behavioral problems, particularly inappropriate sexual behaviors.

❖ Women who report childhood rape are 3 times more likely to become pregnant before age 18.

❖ An estimated 60 Percent of teen first pregnancies are preceded by experiences of molestation, rape, or attempted rape. The average age of their offender is 27 years.

❖ Victims of child sexual abuse are more likely to be sexually promiscuous.

❖ More than 75 Percent of teenage prostitutes have been sexually abused.

❖ Victims of child sexual abuse report more substance abuse problems. Seventy to Eighty Percent of sexual abuse survivors report excessive drug and alcohol use.

❖ Young girls who are sexually abused are 3 times more likely to develop psychiatric disorders or alcohol and drug abuse in adulthood, than girls who are not sexually abused.

# *Identified Issues*

## Primary Causes

1. Emotional, Physical , Sexual and or Mental abuse
2. Lack of parental guidance
3. Lack of active parenting
4. Lack of resources

## Secondary causes

1. Envy
2. Greed
3. Immaturity
4. Mental health issues

## Effects

1. *Promiscuity*
   a. The transmission of Sexual related disease
   b. Lack of knowing one has a disease, in addition to having multiple sexual partners
   c. Knowingly spreading diseases
2. *Rape*
3. *Senseless acts of violence*

## OUTCOME

A continuous vicious cycle, where_babies are having babies resulting in: _The makeup of our society being individuals who lack goals, dreams, ethics, encouragement, self respect education, and self motivation.

# *CALL TO ACTION!!!*

A portion of the proceeds of this books purchase will go towards youth activities geared towards building self esteem; Identifying strengths and contributions within the community. Educational services will be offered on topics such as: Gang Violence; HIV & AIDS awareness; Teen pregnancy; Substance abuse and Mental health.

For more information email: restoration.location@gmail.com

*Let's make a breakthrough restoring what our gutter once took from us*

## **Links to ensure there is support.**

http://www.ncpc.org/topics/gang-voilence-prevention

http://www.rainn.org/get-help/national-sexual-assault-hotline

http://www.glbtnationalhelpcenter.org/

http://kidshealth.org/teen/your_mind/emotions/someone_died.html

http://www.thebody.com/

http://www.cdc.gov/std/general/

http://www.becky-due.com/hot-line-help.html

# References

Browne, A, & Finkelhor, D. (1986). Impact of child sexual abuse: A review of the research. *Psychological Bulletin, 99*, 66-77.

Day, A., Thurlow, K., & Woolliscroft, J. (2003). Working with childhood sexual abuse: A survey of mental health professionals.*Child Abuse & Neglect, 27* , 191-198.

Kendler, K., Bulik, C., Silberg, J., Hettema, J., Myers, J., & Prescott, C. (2000). Childhood sexual abuse and adult psychiatric and substance use disorders in women: An epidemiological and Cotwin Control Analysis. *Archives of General Psychiatry, 57*, 953-959.

Noll, J.G., Trickett, P.K., & Putnam, F.W. (2003). A prospective investigation of the impact of childhood sexual abuse on the development of sexuality . *Journal of Consulting and Clinical Psychology, 71*, 575-586.

Paolucci, E.O, Genuis, M.L, & Violato, C. (2001). A meta-analysis of the published research on the effects of child sexual abuse.*Journal of Psychology* , *135*, 17-36.

Saewyc, E.M., Magee, L.L., & Pettingall, S.E. (2004). Teenage pregnancy and associated risk behavior among sexually abused adolescents. Perspectives on Sexual and Reproductive Health , *36*(3), 98-105.

Voeltanz, N., Wilsnack, S., Harris, R., Wilsnack, R., Wonderlich, S., Kristjanson, A. (1999). Prevalence and risk for childhood sexual abuse in women : National survey findings.. *Child*

21998454R00032

Made in the USA
Charleston, SC
10 September 2013